First Grade
DROPOUT

Written by Audrey Vernick • Illustrated by Matthew Cordell

CLARION BOOKS
Houghton Mifflin Harcourt   Boston   New York

For Jennifer Greene,
the wonderful editor and friend I found
when another wonderful editor dropped out
—A.V.

To Gloria and Al
—M.C.

Clarion Books
3 Park Avenue, 19th Floor,
New York, New York 10016
Text copyright © 2015 by Audrey Vernick
Illustrations copyright © 2015 by Matthew Cordell
Clarion Books is an imprint of Houghton Mifflin Harcourt Publishing Company.
www.hmhco.com
The illustrations in this book were done in pen and ink with watercolor.
The text was set in Amasis MT Std.
Library of Congress Cataloging-in-Publication Data
Vernick, Audrey.
First grade dropout / Audrey Vernick ; illustrated by Matthew Cordell.
pages cm
Summary: After an embarrassing incident, a young boy decides to never return to school.
ISBN 978-0-544-12985-6 (hardcover)
[1. Schools—Fiction. 2. Embarrassment—Fiction. 3. Humorous stories.]
I. Cordell, Matthew, 1975- illustrator. II. Title.
PZ7.V5973Fi 2015
[E]—dc23
2014021780
Manufactured in China
SCP 10 9 8 7 6 5
4500682973

I've been lots of things.

Hungry.

Four years old.

Crazy bored.

Soaking wet.

Wrapped up like a mummy in toilet paper. (Don't ask.)

But the worst thing to be is what I am now. I call it

There is no way I can go back to Lakeview Elementary School tomorrow.

Here's something you might not know about me:
If I saw something embarrassing happen to someone,
there is no way I would laugh.

I did something embarrassing today, and my best friend, Tyler, laughed. Everyone laughed.

So now I need a plan.

I know!

I'll wear my floppy black magic hat

and cast a spell that unsays what I said.

Or—this makes more sense—I could build a time machine
and go back to before this all happened.

Maybe I'll just put on glasses and change my hair and
pretend to be a new kid from . . .

London.   Or France.   Or Cincinnati.

I can't stop thinking about it.

How everyone laughed and slapped their desks and stomped their feet.

And pointed. At me.

Okay, so maybe last year I laughed by accident when
Tyler's turtle costume fell off.
But that was FUNNY.
And the next day Tyler was still at school.
I wonder if he tried the time-machine idea.

Anyway, what happened to me was worse.

I raised my hand.

I waited my turn.

And when Ms. Morgan called on me . . .

. . . I accidentally . . . called her . . .

I. Called. My. Teacher.

MOMMY!!!

It was quiet. Then it started, all at once,
like a big marching band of laughing people.

So that's that.

I'm not going back. Goodbye, Lakeview Elementary!

I am a first grade dropout.

It'll be fine. I'll stay at home for a bunch of years, no big deal,
work on my jump shot, and maybe when I'm a teenager,
I'll get a job. (My parents have not yet agreed to this plan.)

old me

I'll have to make new friends.
But I really like the friends I already have.

I'll miss playing basketball
with Emma.

Spying on Tyler's sisters
from the treehouse.

Fishing with Levon and his uncle.

But they all laughed.
And stomped their
feet. And pointed.

Ms. Morgan didn't laugh. She said, "Don't worry. It happens every year."

Easy for her to say.

Ms. Morgan never had a whole marching band of laughing happen to her.

Walking to soccer, I realize I'll have to drop out of *everything*.

There's Tyler laughing with Charley and Levon.

Still laughing.

I hide behind the goal.

Not a great choice.

Tyler spots me and comes right over.

I put my hand on my hip, like someone who doesn't care if other people laugh.

I hold my breath.

I wait for Tyler to laugh.

"Hey," Tyler says, like it's a regular day.

"Hey," I say, blowing out my held-in breath.

I tell him my plan. "I'm dropping out."

"Of what?"

"School," I say.

"Awesome," Tyler says. "I'll drop out too." He high-fives me.

"It'll be great! We can work on our junk shots."

A laugh tries to burst right out of my mouth.

I press my hand over my lips to keep it in.

I close my eyes tight.

"What are you doing?" Tyler asks.

"Not laughing," I say through my fingers.

"What are you not laughing at?" he asks.

I open one eye.

"It's not *junk* shot. It's *jump* shot."

"Oh," Tyler says.

I open my other eye.

He looks like he looked when his turtle costume fell off.

And then he laughs.

"But 'junk shot' sounds awesome," I say.

"We should totally invent a junk shot together."

"At recess tomorrow?"

"Definitely," I say.

"Maybe we can show it to Ms. Morgan. I mean . . .